The
Recital

The Recital

AND OTHER FRIENDSHIP AND FAMILY STORIES
Compiled by the Editors
of
Highlights for Children

Compilation copyright © 1995 by Highlights for Children, Inc.
Contents copyright by Highlights for Children, Inc.
Published by Highlights for Children, Inc.
P.O. Box 18201
Columbus, Ohio 43218-0201
Printed in the United States of America

ISBN 0-87534-662-6

Highlights is a registered trademark of Highlights for Children, Inc.

CONTENTS

The Recital

By Genna S. White

Amy frowned at the piano. This was the hardest section of the song. She had to concentrate as her fingers moved over the black and white piano keys. She breathed a sigh of relief when she finished. Only one mistake.

"Good work, Amy," Mrs. Baxter said as she glanced at her watch. "That's it for today. Next time, plan to stay an extra half-hour, OK? I want you and Jonathan to be here together so we can work on your duet."

Amy nodded and gathered up her music books. As she went outside into the sunshine, her friend Jonathan pedaled up on his bicycle and slammed to a stop.

"Hi, Jonathan," Amy said.

"Hi," he said. "I guess I'm late for my lesson."

"No, I just finished. And guess what? Mrs. Baxter wants to listen to our duet next time."

Jonathan grinned. "That's great! I think she'll be pretty impressed."

"I don't know." Amy hesitated. "I'd feel better if we practiced some more."

"How about this afternoon?"

"Good idea."

"Let's meet at my house," Jonathan said. "I'll be home in about an hour."

"See you then," Amy said, waving good-bye as Jonathan rushed through the doors of the music hall for his lesson.

Amy quickly walked the two blocks to her house, her music books tucked under her arm. The piano recital was only a couple of weeks away, and Amy was excited. She had been practicing hard, learning her solo pieces. And she and Jonathan got together often to work on their duet. Since Jonathan's house was right behind Amy's, it was easy to arrange times to practice.

"Hi, Dad," Amy said, walking into the kitchen when she got home.

Her father was kneeling on the floor in front of the cabinets, a paintbrush in his hand. He looked up and smiled. "How was your lesson?"

"Terrific. Jonathan and I are going to practice our duet when he gets home this afternoon."

"Over here?" Her father brushed paint across a cabinet door.

"His house this time," Amy said. She glanced around the room. "This color is pretty. Do you want me to help paint?"

"Sure. Grab a brush."

The minutes flew by as Amy and her father painted. Suddenly, Amy realized what time it was and jumped to her feet. *Jonathan should be home by now,* she thought.

"I'll be back later," Amy told her father.

She went outside and ran to the chain link fence that separated her yard from Jonathan's. Jonathan was standing by his back door.

"I thought you forgot," Jonathan called. "I was about to come get you."

Amy started to climb over the fence. "I didn't forget. I was helping—"

Just then, the toe of Amy's sneaker got caught on the top of the fence. She wobbled for a moment, trying to get her balance, but it was no use. She fell hard on the ground in Jonathan's yard.

"Amy!" Jonathan ran over. "Are you OK?"

Tears stung Amy's eyes. "My arm's hurt!"

"Don't move. I'll get your dad."

In a minute, Amy's father was there, examining her arm. "I think we should take you to the emergency clinic, honey."

"Is she going to be OK?" Jonathan asked.

"She'll be fine," Amy's father said. "But I want a doctor to look at that arm. They can take x rays at the clinic."

"X rays?" Amy looked at her father. "Do you think my arm is broken?"

"It could be, Amy."

And it was. Amy came back home with a cast on her left arm.

"What are you going to do about the recital?" Jonathan asked the next day when he signed Amy's cast. "It's in two weeks."

Amy shook her head. "I guess I can't perform in it," she sighed.

"That's too bad."

"Yeah," Amy said softly. She stared at the bulky cast on her arm. It wasn't fair. She knew there would be other recitals, but she had been looking forward to this one. Amy loved the music she would be playing, and this was the first time she had ever played in a duet.

"Well, at least it was your left arm that got hurt," Jonathan said.

"What do you mean?"

He gestured at Amy's arm. "You're right-handed. Just think how hard it would be to do things if your right arm were broken."

"Oh. I guess you're right."

Jonathan nodded. "I bet there's a lot that you can do with just your right hand."

Amy stared at him. "I can even play the piano with one hand, can't I?"

"I guess so."

A grin slowly spread across Amy's face. "There's no way that I can play my solo pieces in the recital, but what about our duet? Do you think there's a way that I could play our song with only one hand?"

"If we change some of the notes around, and I played some of your part . . . " Jonathan smiled and shrugged. "It's worth a shot. Let's work on it. We'll see what we can do."

The day of the recital, Amy was nervous and excited. She watched the other piano students as they took the stage, and listened to them play their solos and duets. She felt a twinge of sadness because she couldn't perform her solo pieces. But at least she would be in the recital.

Finally, it was Amy's turn. She and Jonathan walked to the stage and sat down at the piano. Amy glanced out into the audience and smiled at her parents. Then she and Jonathan began to play.

Amy and Jonathan performed their duet, the same song they had practiced for weeks. But there was a difference. Amy was playing with only her right hand. With Jonathan's help, she had found a way to be in the recital.

The audience broke into applause at the end of the song, and Amy grinned. Jonathan gently poked her in the ribs.

"We didn't sound so bad, did we?" he whispered.

"We sounded great," Amy said softly, smiling into the crowd. "Just great."

Room
Enough
for Two

By Carolyn Bowman

Jackson and Lyla got along as well as two fish in a rain barrel, until the day their parents bought the new refrigerator. It was delivered on a truck, in a box. . . .

"As big as a cave!" said Jackson, who liked to run wild in the woods behind their house while hunting for woolly mammoths.

"As big as a castle!" said Lyla, who dreamed that she was a beautiful princess, ruler of a vast and loyal kingdom.

"I saw it first," said Jackson. "I claim dibs."

"No, it's mine!" said Lyla. "That box is going to be my castle."

"My cave!" Jackson argued.

"You both saw it at the same time," said their mother. "There's room enough for two."

And so began the battle of the box.

Jackson licked his lips as the movers lowered the refrigerator off the truck and onto the drive-way. Already his cave was taking shape. The front entrance would be carved into an arch. He would paint his cave brown, with green leaves, so that it wouldn't show in the woods, where he planned to keep it.

There would be a secret escape hatch at the back of his cave, one that would open and close. A caveman might need to escape in a hurry, especially if a wild animal were lurking around. He glanced sideways at Lyla.

Lyla brought her hands together and breathed into them, something she did when she was very excited. The movers were uncrating the refrigerator. "Be careful!" she said. "That box is my castle."

"My cave!" said Jackson, and their father frowned.

"Please, be careful," Lyla said.

"Yes, please," said Jackson politely, and their father smiled.

Lyla ran into the house for her crayons. Already she could see her castle, the tallest one in the kingdom. She would give it tiny windows so that she could see out but no one else could see in, especially Jackson. She would draw a turret. No castle was complete without a turret, the place where princesses went to hide out. Again she thought of Jackson. Well, maybe she'd let him visit once in a while.

Lyla and Jackson waved good-bye to the delivery men, then . . .

"Mine!" said Jackson, and he claimed the box for himself.

"Mine!" said Lyla, grabbing one flap and pulling it several inches.

"Mine!" said their mother, firmly putting her hand on the box. "And it will stay mine until you find a way to share. May I suggest a meeting— over a picnic lunch—where you can calmly discuss your ideas?"

With lunch spread before them on the backyard picnic table, Jackson and Lyla continued to glare at each other.

"If it were a castle," Lyla said, "we could have grand parties." She bit into a dill pickle and returned her brother's frown. "You could pretend to be the evil knight, attack my castle, and try to take it for your own." But she knew she'd never let him win.

Jackson took a bite of his sandwich. "If it were a cave, we could go on hunts."

"I don't like hunting," Lyla said.

"You could hunt for berries and stuff like that." Jackson stopped. He didn't really know that much about what cave people did. "We could have a camp-out. We could sing songs, and count stars, and look for constellations."

"We could do that," Lyla said, "in a castle."

"Oh, Lyla, you always have to have your own way!" Jackson said angrily.

"Says who?"

"Says me!"

That ended the argument. Lunch was finished. They carried their leftovers into the kitchen, then sat, dreaming their dreams, near the refrigerator box.

Just then Holly came by. Holly lived next door, and she was always bragging. "I'm going to a play—a real, live play," she said. "There will be actors and actresses on a big stage. They'll sing and dance and make up stories. Too bad you can't come."

Jackson and Lyla looked at one another, then at the refrigerator box.

"A play!" said Jackson.

"Yeah! It could be different each time," Lyla added, her eyes as big as half-dollars. "And a play needs a stage."

"A different kind of stage each time," Jackson said. "We wouldn't draw on the stage, just draw on paper, to put on the stage."

"And we could use leaves and branches and rocks and stuff," Lyla said.

Jackson looked at Holly, then at his sister. "We could charge admission."

"Five cents," said Lyla.

"What are you guys talking about?" asked Holly.

Jackson and Lyla weren't saying. They just looked at each other, happy to share at last.

Paper Hearts

By Heather Klassen

"My mom said I could get that large box of valentines in the card shop window," Rebecca announces to us.

"That box must cost ten dollars," Aubrey says. "My mom would never go for that."

"My mom understands how important it is to give out special valentines," Rebecca replies.

"I'll have to just get a box of regular ones," Aubrey says. "The kind with the funny sayings. What kind are you giving out, Molly?"

Rebecca and Aubrey turn toward me, waiting for my answer. The image of my mother hunched over the kitchen table muttering about electric bills and new shoes flashes into my mind. Boxed valentines? I know exactly what Mom would say if I asked her. She'd sigh and say, "Molly, it's been a tough year. My paycheck just isn't stretching far enough. And they raised the taxes again. But I'm sure we have some red construction paper somewhere."

My friends are waiting for my answer. I shrug and say, "I don't know yet."

"The older we get, the fancier the valentines are," Rebecca says. "Isn't it great? Even the ones from the boys are getting better."

The bell saves me from further discussion of valentine cards. But in class we work on covering shoeboxes with doilies and glitter. Everyone talks about the party on Friday. Some of the boys grumble about Valentine's Day, but they're also whispering into friends' ears about the fancy cards they'll buy for the girls they kind of like, I'm sure. The more expensive the better.

"Ow!" I cry, accidently jabbing my thumb with my scissors. Stupid valentine box. Stupid party.

After school, I avoid Rebecca and Aubrey and walk home alone. I pass the card shop, stare in the window, then keep going. A block later, I stop, retrace my steps, and go into the store. It couldn't hurt to look.

I finger the boxes of cards in the valentine aisle, flipping them over to check the prices. Nothing under six dollars. I know how much six dollars can buy at the grocery store. I know my mother would never agree to buy these cards. And I know I'll be the only one in class who doesn't hand out store-bought cards. Just as I'm the only one in class who can never go out for pizza on Friday afternoons or meet at the mall or the roller rink on Saturdays. I'm the only one in class always left out. Sometimes I'm surprised that my friends stick with me at all.

No, I could never buy these cards, I think as I stare at the box I'm holding. *But I could . . . take them?* My fingers shake. I almost drop the box, not believing I even thought that. But the store is busy, and no one would notice. Just this once. Then I'd have cards like everyone else.

I glance up and see Rebecca charging around the end of the aisle.

"Molly! Are those the cards you're buying?"

I jam the box onto the shelf. "No," I reply, my cheeks burning.

"Then what were you doing with them?" Rebecca asks. She stares at me. "Were you . . . "

"No money," I say, backing down the aisle. I get out of there, fast.

I hurry down the sidewalk, my backpack slapping my shoulder blades. "I wouldn't have taken the cards," I tell myself, whether Rebecca had shown up or not. But I thought it. That's bad enough.

I avoid all discussions of valentine cards for the next few days. Thursday night I find the red construction paper and cut hearts out of it. I print my classmates' names on one side and my name on the other. We don't have any glitter or ribbons. *So that's it,* I think as I shove the valentines into my backpack.

I get to school early Friday to distribute my cards. I don't watch as the others slip theirs through the slits on the box tops. I start counting the hours until the day will be over.

"It's time!" Rebecca calls at 2:15, reminding Mr. Vargas to start the party. We eat heart-shaped candy and drink red punch. And open valentine cards. The pile on my desk grows, the envelopes fluttering to the floor. Beautiful cards, funny cards—all nice, none homemade. I thank my friends for their cards, they thank me for mine. But I'm sure they don't really mean it.

Then I spot Rebecca and Aubrey. Rebecca's holding my card and whispering to Aubrey. *My best friends,* I think, *laughing at my cards.* Tears threaten my eyes, but I blink them back.

Aubrey returns to her desk, rummages around, and comes up with my card. I sink lower into my seat, wondering what they're doing. Wondering if I really have any friends at all.

Rebecca and Aubrey march over to the bulletin board Mr. Vargas decorated for the party. It has "My Favorite Valentine" at the top and a space under everyone's name where each student can post the best card he or she received. The board is already covered with glittery, store-bought cards.

Rebecca and Aubrey each take a tack and the card I handed out, and they pin them up. My construction paper cards are their favorite valentines.

My friends turn and smile at me, and suddenly I know something. I may be left out of lots of things, things that cost money. But I'm not left out of what's important. I smile back at my friends, wishing I could tell them how my heart feels right now.

Backyard Neighbors

By Judy Cox

Mike flattened himself against the floor of his tree fort, high up in the leafy branches of a big maple. He peered through a crack in the boards and glared at the new person. He could see gray in the woman's hair as she walked beneath the tree fort. He lay still as a mouse, holding his breath. But she never looked up.

The house behind Mike had been empty for years, ever since Mike could remember. But today—the worst day of Mike's life—a new owner was moving in.

After she left, Mike scrambled down from his fort. He wriggled under the hedge separating his yard from the new lady's. He yanked open his kitchen door, letting it slam behind him.

The smell of baking cookies greeted him. Mike grabbed a couple from the counter.

"Mike," Mom said, picking a twig out of his hair, "you've been in the tree fort again, haven't you? And after I told you!" Mike took a bite and chewed, waiting for the lecture.

"I built it," he said, swallowing. "It's *my* fort."

"Not anymore," said Mom. "I told you. That tree isn't ours. Our yard ends at the hedge. I know I shouldn't have let you play over there, but our yard is just so small. . . . " She sighed. "Now that we have a neighbor living there, you have to stay in our yard. You are *not* to go in that tree fort anymore. I want you to promise that you won't."

Mike's eyes stung. He couldn't give up his fort. Mom saw his face and reached out to hug him. "I know what the fort means to you, honey. Can't you build one in our yard?" Mike pulled away and shook his head. There weren't any trees in his yard. That's why he built the fort next door in the first place.

Mom piled cookies on a plate. Mike reached for another, but she tapped his hand. "Take these to our new neighbor," she said. "And Mike . . ." He turned, holding the plate. "Be nice!"

The lady he had seen before opened the door. "I'm Nita," she said. She shook Mike's hand with a strong grip. Little wrinkles curled up around her warm brown eyes. She thanked Mike for the cookies and invited him in. As they sat around the table, she talked about her plans to fix up her yard.

Mike listened with a sinking heart.

Over the next few weeks, Mike kept his promise to stay out of the tree fort. He stayed in his room, watching Nita work in her yard, right under his fort. She mowed the weeds, spaded up dirt, planted flowers. Once Nita looked up, saw Mike, and waved. Mike turned away.

Soon the yard lost its wild look. Mike watched, fascinated in spite of himself. One day, Nita brought out some boxes, like little wooden houses, and set them up. She hung long tubes from the branches of Mike's tree and filled them with seeds. She put up a birdbath, filling it from her hose.

The following week, birdsong woke Mike. He hurried to the window. Birds were everywhere, fluttering in the trees, scratching on the ground, splashing in the water. Some of the birds had black heads, like little caps. Some birds were yellow.

Mike leaned out the window. Nita came outside, a brown bag in each hand. "Hi!" she called
to Mike. "Did you see the goldfinches?" She held
up a bag and laughed. "They've eaten all the this-
tle seed, greedy things. I'm filling the feeder
again. Want to help?"

"OK," Mike said. A moment later he squirmed
under the hedge and into Nita's yard.

"Here," Nita said, handing him a sack. She pried
off the feeder lid and showed Mike how to fill it
with tiny black seeds. "Goldfinches eat this. Chickadees and juncoes eat sunflower seeds." She
handed him the other sack.

"Goldfinches," said Mike. "Are those the yellow ones?"

"Yes," said Nita. "The chickadees have black
caps. They say their own name, you know." She
called, "*Chicka-dee-dee-dee! Chicka-dee-dee-
dee!*" A sputter of calls answered from the trees.
Mike laughed.

"Do you know the names of all the birds?"

"Not all," said Nita. "but I know a lot of them.
Are you interested in birds?"

"I don't know," said Mike. "They look pretty cool."

"I'll lend you a book that tells their names."
Nita saw a big marmalade cat under the hedge.
She clapped her hands. The cat bounded off. "I

don't know what I'm going to do about the cats," she sighed.

Mike watched the birds every day. Mom found an old pair of binoculars, and he learned to tell the chickadees from the juncoes.

But even with binoculars, he couldn't see well. His bedroom window was too high. He'd read about bird photographers building blinds to get close while taking pictures. The tree fort would be a perfect blind.

The next day, Mike crawled under the hedge and scrambled into his fort. The birds flew away, but Mike kept still, and one by one they flew back.

Mike could see every feather. He watched for hours. Then he spotted someone else watching, too. The marmalade cat slipped through the bushes, sneaking up on a junco scratching for seeds in the dirt. The cat put his chin on his paws, stuck his tail up, and wiggled his rump.

"Scat!" Mike clapped his hands. The birds took wing with cries of alarm. The cat gave Mike a narrow look and slunk away.

Mike sighed with relief, but then he saw Nita watching him. He was trespassing. Would she be angry? Would she tell Mom? He slid down.

"Good job, Mike!" said Nita. "I've had more trouble with cats! I wish I knew what to do."

"I could keep the cats away," offered Mike. "Why don't I come over every day and use the tree fort for bird watching?"

"That's a great idea, Mike. You can be my official bird guard!"

"Bird guard," laughed Mike. He'd tell Mom how Nita had a bird security system, the birds had a backyard sanctuary, and he had his tree fort back.

Checkers

By Betty Bates

Gramps and Gram played this really vicious game of checkers. In summer, they'd sit at the table in front of the electric fan, and Gram would say, "There! I gotcha, old man."

Then Gramps would say, "No, you don't, old lady." He'd jump three of her men in a row, and she'd have to crown his king.

In winter, they'd sit in front of the fire. Gramps would say, "Ha! I've got you cornered, old lady."

And Gram would say, "Think you're pretty cute, don't you?" Then she'd jump her way out of the corner.

Last week, Gramps died. He just didn't wake up one morning.

All of a sudden Gram was quiet. She hardly spoke at all. At the memorial service, I sat next to her. I kept my hand on top of her freckled one the whole time.

The next day, I put on my jacket and my hat and my scarf and my boots and my mittens. I tramped through the deep snow down the road past the cornfield to her house. She was sitting at the table in front of the cold fireplace, all hunched over, staring at a spot on the wall. I took off my mittens and my boots and my scarf and my hat and my jacket.

"Hi, Gram," I said.

"Hi, Seth," she said.

That's all. Just "Hi, Seth." She didn't even smile at me. She kept staring at that spot.

The house was scary quiet.

I didn't know what to do. I didn't want to bother Gram. So I put on my jacket and my hat and my scarf and my boots and my mittens and went back home.

The next day, I put on my jacket and my hat and my scarf and my boots and my mittens. I tramped through deeper snow down the road to Gram's place.

She was sitting at the table in front of the cold fireplace, staring at the same spot. All she said was, "Hi, Seth." She didn't smile at me.

So I put on my things and went home.

The same thing happened each day last week. The snow got deeper, and still deeper.

Gram never smiled at me.

What could I do?

This morning I put on my jacket and my hat and my scarf and my boots and my mittens and fought my way through the snow to Gram's house. "Hi, Gram," I said. I took off my mittens and, very carefully, I lit the fire Gramps had laid before he died. I went up behind Gram, put my arms around her neck, rubbed my cheek against hers, and got her wet with the snow from my jacket. "I'm sorry about Gramps," I said. "I miss him, too."

Gram sighed. She reached up and patted my hand. "Thank you, Seth," she said with a sniffle.

She pulled out a tissue and wiped tears and melted snow from her face. She took a deep breath and straightened up in her chair. She picked up the checkerboard, opened it, and slapped it down on the table. "Don't just stand there, young man. Take off your things, and let's get going."

While the fire crackled and sparkled and kept us warm, she beat me. "There, young fella," she said as she jumped my last man. "I gotcha."

I didn't care.

Because now she was smiling at me.

A Lucky Lass

By Anita Borgo

The warm March breeze chased bunches of dried oak leaves into a spiral. An early spring brought a warm St. Patrick's Day and the season's first soccer practice.

Helen expertly dribbled the soccer ball through the deserted park on her way home from soccer practice. To celebrate the holiday, her team went to Shamrock Sam's for green french fries and minty shakes. Helen didn't join them. She couldn't think of her stomach with so many thoughts in her head.

How could Coach Kelly bench me? she thought. *I'm the best player on the Cardinals, the girls' soccer team. I can dribble, score, and defend better than anyone.*

"Play your position and pass the ball, Helen," Coach Kelly had said. "This is a team sport. Play like you're part of the team or don't play."

Maggie knows I'm the best player.

"Everyone knows you scored the most goals," Maggie, her best friend, had said. "You don't have to brag about it."

My older sister wishes she could kick as hard as I can.

"I'm trying my best," Denise had said when Helen asked why the ball fell short of the goal. "I don't have the power you have."

Even Beth, the new girl, knows I'm the star.

"You could win the game single-handedly," she had said.

Why doesn't Coach Kelly realize the Cardinals need me?

Helen juggled the ball a dozen times before missing. It bounced sideways off her knee and rolled under some bushes. She knelt down, peering through the thick branches. She spotted the familiar black-and-white pattern nestled in some curled leaves.

A low grunt sounded from behind the ball. Helen watched as the ball rolled to the side. Her eyes widened as she discovered who had shoved it.

"If that's not the size of the Blarney Stone, I'm not Conner O'Leary." A man the size of a cucumber wiped his palms on the seat of his dark green jeans. He wore an emerald green baseball cap, electric green high-tops, and a lime green T-shirt with the words "Kiss me, I'm Irish" printed across the front. He looked like a sporty pickle.

St. Patrick's Day, leprechaun, and *pot of gold* swept through Helen's mind as she reached to swoop up the tiny man. As her fingers closed around him, he leaped forward and wrapped his arms around her thumb.

"Gotcha!" they both shouted.

"I caught you first," Helen argued. She tried to stand to make her point, but stumbled.

The little man bent back her finger.

"Ouch! Stop that. I didn't hurt you," she cried.

He braced himself against a branch of the bush and tugged harder. "If I let you go, no one will ever believe Conner O'Leary caught a human on St. Patrick's Day."

"No one will believe *you,* because *you didn't.* I caught a leprechaun on St. Patrick's Day, and you're going to make me rich."

Mr. O'Leary released his hold, slapped his knee, and chuckled. His laugh sounded like chirping crickets. Helen pulled away her hand.

"Whoever . . . whoever told you that story?" he asked between bouts of giggles.

Helen sat cross-legged. "It's something that everybody knows. If you catch a leprechaun on St. Patrick's Day, he'll lead you to a pot of gold and make you rich. But a leprechaun is also tricky." She rubbed her thumb. "He might pretend that he caught you instead of the other way around."

Conner leaned against the soccer ball. "My people tell a different version of the story. If you catch a human on March 17, he or she will grant three wishes. You're a human, I caught you, and I want my wishes."

Helen folded her arms. "I want my gold."

The man scratched his head and studied Helen's face. "We have a wee bit of a problem here, lass. With luck, it'll all work out. I'm a simple man as you can see by my simple dress. My wishes are only to make the world a better place for humans and leprechauns. I wish for a friend's smile, a sister's nod, and a teammate's good wishes. If you grant me that, I'll give you wealth."

Helen and Mr. O'Leary shook hand and finger and agreed to meet at the same time tomorrow.

At soccer practice, Helen concentrated on playing her halfback position. During the scrimmage, Helen had a clear shot at the goal. She only needed to move up. Remembering Coach Kelly's advice, she passed the ball to Maggie. Maggie dribbled into position, fired the ball, and scored. Her grin flashed like a sparkling coin.

At break, Helen showed her sister how to use the inside of her foot for an accurate power kick.

Denise listened, practiced a few kicks, and nodded in agreement. "Thanks for the hint."

A tinkling like a pocketful of change tickled Helen's ears.

Helen played goalie the last quarter but didn't see much action. The new girl, Beth, played so well the ball never got near the goal. "You'll do great in Saturday's game," said Helen. For a moment, a rainbow arched above the park even though it hadn't rained.

Coach Kelly called Helen aside. "On Saturday, you'll start at forward. Great teamwork today."

After practice, the Cardinals gathered at Beth's house for pizza. Helen promised to meet them later. She had an appointment to keep.

Moments later she found the bushes and looked for Mr. O'Leary. His head popped out of a hole the soccer ball had covered yesterday.

"There you are. I granted your wishes," she said.

Mr. O'Leary heaved himself out of his burrow and stared into her face. "Come closer, lass."

Helen leaned forward. She felt his gentle hands on her cheeks as he gazed into her eyes.

"Aye, I see that you have. And is the world a better place today?"

Helen thought of her friend Maggie, her sister Denise, her teammate Beth, Coach Kelly, and all the Cardinals. "Yes, it is, and I believe you owe me a pot of gold."

"Ah, I promised wealth, not gold. You've found the wealth of friendship. That's more valuable than all the coins in Ireland." With a twist of his baseball cap, Mr. O'Leary disappeared.

Helen knew she was a lucky lass to be tricked into becoming a better friend.

The Bargain

By Jean E. Doyle

Jonas kicked a stone into the street. "I wish we didn't have school today," he said. "I didn't get my math homework done, and I can't think of a good excuse."

"No excuse would be a good one," said his friend Marcie. "Miss Parker says she's heard them all. You'd better just tell her you didn't do it and ask her if you can do it tonight."

"But we'll probably get more math today. How can I do two assignments when I can barely get through one?" Jonas felt trapped.

They walked along in silence for half a block, then Marcie had an idea. "We'll get to school early this morning. Why don't you go to a quiet corner of the playground and do it there?"

"But we're going to have a basketball game," Jonas protested. "Our class has a good chance of beating the other fifth grade, and our team needs all the players it can get. I promised I'd play, and the guys are counting on me." He was one of his class's best players.

"Then you'd better start hoping for some luck," Marcie joked. "Miss Parker gets pretty upset when people don't do their homework. You will definitely be in trouble if you don't turn in your assignment today."

Jonas kicked another stone so hard it went all the way across the street and up onto the sidewalk. A squirrel quickly jumped out of the way and scolded angrily from a low branch.

When they reached the corner by the candy store, Jonas thought of a way out of his predicament. "Marcie," he said slowly, "would you do my math assignment for me? I'll give you my new two-color ballpoint pen if you do."

She looked at him and slowly shook her head. "I already have one. Besides, doing that math page once was enough for me. It took me more than a half hour to get it done. I even had to miss ten minutes of my favorite TV show."

"But you'd only have to make a copy of your paper for me," Jonas coaxed. "That would just take you five minutes. Just remember to write kind of sloppy like I do. Miss Parker won't notice. Then I can play in this game."

"Sorry," Marcie answered. "Why should I do your homework for you? Nobody did mine for me."

Jonas was getting desperate. "I'll do your science homework for you tonight if you do."

He was good at science, and Marcie knew it. She'd always found science difficult and frustrating, and it would be a relief not to have to do the workbook pages Miss Parker always assigned for Wednesday night. The offer was a tempting one.

Jonas found it hard not to smile as he waited for her to make up her mind. Surely it was an offer she couldn't refuse.

But she did. "Sorry," she said again. "I've got other things to do besides your homework." She walked off quickly to meet her other friends.

Jonas was stunned. Now what could he do? Over by the basketball hoop he could hear some boys shouting and calling his name. The game was about to begin.

Derek ran up to him. "Come on, hurry up!" he urged. "We've only got half an hour to play. What took you so long?"

Jonas gripped his books so tightly that his hand hurt. He swallowed hard and said, "I can't play this morning, Derek. There's something I have to do. Maybe I can play after school."

"But that'll be too late!" Derek objected. "We need to have the game before school, not after. Are you scared you'll miss a few shots?"

Jonas shuffled his feet and didn't answer. Derek angrily turned away and ran back to join the others under the hoop.

Jonas found a quiet place by the corner of the building far away from the other children. He sat down on a large rock and opened his math book. He stared at the math page and then began to work out the first problem. Marcie was right—this wasn't easy work. He might not be able to do it all in half an hour.

After ten long minutes he had completed only three problems. Then suddenly he was aware of someone standing near him. He looked up into Marcie's face.

"Hi," she said. "Do you need some help?"

"I sure do," he answered. "I'm stuck on number four." He stared at his book.

She sat down beside him, and together they worked out the rest of the assignment. But Marcie insisted that he do his own work, and when he was finished they compared their answers.

"I got them all right!" Jonas exclaimed. "That NEVER happened before."

"Maybe you just never worked this hard before," she laughed.

"You know, you're right," he agreed. "I've always made such a big deal about math homework. Maybe that's why it always seemed so hard."

They walked toward the school door just as the bell sounded and the basketball game stopped. Hordes of children scrambled for the entrance.

"By the way," said Marcie, "that science report we have to finish by the end of this month—I could use a little help. Do you know anybody who's good at science?"

"Maybe I can find someone," Jonas grinned. "Only one thing . . . "

"What?"

"This guy would expect you to do all of your own work."

"No problem," she answered. "Just so I get help over the rough spots."

Suddenly they were surrounded by the basketball players from both fifth grades.

"Hey, Jonas," Derek shouted, "the score is tied. How about joining us after school to finish the game? We could use another good player."

"You've got one," Jonas grinned.

The Hudson Street Gang

By Mary E. Furlong

"Rickety-rackety-rackety-bang. That's how they know we're the Hudson Street gang."

Eddie watched them from the front steps of the apartment building—a half dozen big kids, their arms linked together so that they looked like a wall of people moving along Hudson Street. "Rickety-rackety-rackety-bang. That's how they know we're the Hudson Street gang."

A man sweeping the sidewalk in front of Rizzo's Food Market leaned on his broom handle and

watched them go by. From a window on the sec-
ond floor above Frank's Fashion Footwear, a
jolly-looking woman laughed and waved. A little
boy steered his three-wheeler in a big circle right
in front of the gang just to show them that they
couldn't scare him.

"Rickety-rackety-rackety-bang. That's how they
know . . . Hey, look. There's the new kid."

The gang stopped on the sidewalk right in front
of Eddie. "Hey, kid," called a tall skinny girl with a
ponytail. "What's your name?"

Eddie looked down at his sneakers. One of his
laces had come undone. Good. He could concentrate on tying it until the gang went by. If he
kept his head down, they wouldn't see how
scared he was.

"Hey, kid," called the girl again. Eddie didn't
look up. After a moment, someone laughed. Then
they started off down the street again. "Rickety-
rackety-rackety-bang. That's how they know we're
the Hudson Street gang."

"I hate Hudson Street," Eddie murmured to himself. "Why did we have to move here?"

He knew the answer, of course. He and Mom
couldn't afford to go on living in the Riverside
section of town, where the rents were high and
you had to have a car in order to get around.

Hudson Street had smaller, older apartments that didn't cost so much. And there were a lot of stores in the neighborhood, where Mom could do most of her shopping. The school bus stopped right around the corner. Eddie could walk there by himself while Mom got an early start to her job at the bank downtown.

"They don't sound scary to me," Mom said when Eddie told her about the Hudson Street gang. "They're just kids having fun. Maybe some of them are third-graders just like you. You can make friends with them next week, when you start at your new school."

She smiled as she said it, but Eddie could see the worry lines in her forehead. He could tell that Mom wasn't any happier about the move to Hudson Street than he was.

"Sure," he said, trying to sound cheerful. He didn't look forward to going to the new school— not when it meant riding on the bus with the noisy Hudson Street gang.

Eddie didn't see the gang when he arrived at the school bus stop on Monday morning. But lots of other kids were there—little ones mostly—from Pear Avenue, and Twenty-ninth Street, and the housing project over near the park. They laughed and yelled and jumped up and down as they waited for the bus to come. Eddie stood off by himself, checking his jacket pocket from time to time, to make sure that he hadn't lost his lunch money or the transfer paper from the old school on Riverside Drive.

Suddenly, someone screamed. The laughing and yelling stopped. Eddie looked up just in time to see a really big kid—one he'd never seen before—grabbing a little girl's lunch box. "Gimme that," said the big kid. "Let's see if there's any money inside."

Eddie looked around. Surely, some older boy or girl would help. But besides the mean big kid who was stealing the little girl's lunch box, Eddie himself was the biggest one there.

He took a deep breath. "Leave that little girl alone," he said in a loud voice. He hoped he sounded tough.

The mean kid laughed. "Ha! And who's going to make me?"

Eddie was shaking in his shoes, but he knew that he couldn't back off. Someone had to help the girl with the lunch box. Someone had to look out for all the other little kids, too. He took another deep breath. "I am," he said to the mean kid. His voice sounded shaky, scared.

The mean kid laughed again. He dropped the lunch box and grabbed Eddie's jacket collar, leaning down to stare right into his face. "OK, tough guy," he said. "Show me how you're going to do that."

"You leave him alone," came a voice from behind Eddie. "He belongs to the Hudson Street gang."

It was the tall girl with the ponytail. With her stood the rest of the gang—not just the older ones who liked to march up and down the sidewalk together, but kids of all ages—kindergartners and first-graders and a boy who looked as if he might be in the third grade just like Eddie.

The mean kid let go of Eddie's collar. "I was just fooling with him," he muttered. He shoved his hands into his pockets and peered down the street to see if the bus was coming.

The tall girl looked at the lunch pail, sizing up the situation. "You'll fit right in with the gang," she told Eddie. "Hudson Street kids look out for each other."

Then she told him her name—Joanna—and introduced him to the rest of the gang. "When we get to school, I'll help you find the principal's office," she said. "And you can meet us at the bus stop at the end of the day."

Just then, the school bus came along. "Are you kids going to be the noisiest ones again today?" asked the driver with a grin.

"Right!" shouted the gang, scrambling on board. "Rickety-rackety-rackety-bang," they yelled as the bus made its way toward school. "That's how they know we're the Hudson Street gang."

And Eddie sang out the loudest of them all.

Visiting Aunt Lucy

By Judy Cox

Caleb had just finished his homework when the phone rang. His dog, Shep, snoozed at his feet.

In a minute, Dad came in, worry lines creasing his face. "Pleasant View Care Center called," he said. "Grandpa's missing."

Caleb jumped up from his chair. "How can Grandpa be missing?"

Dad shook his head. "They aren't sure. Sometimes people with Alzheimer's get confused and wander off. That's why we took him there to live in the first place. He just wasn't safe on the farm anymore."

Caleb nodded. He knew Grandpa didn't always recognize his family or friends. He remembered the day Grandpa left the stove on and the potholder caught fire, and the time he drank a bottle of cough syrup, thinking it was juice. Grandpa couldn't take care of himself, and with Dad at work all day and Caleb in school, there hadn't been any other choice. Pleasant View Care Center seemed like the best place for him.

But now Grandpa was missing. "The Center called the police," Dad was saying. "They've contacted the newspaper and TV in case someone sees him." He rubbed his hand over his face. "Come on, let's drive around and see if we can spot him."

Caleb whistled to Shep, and they got in the car with Dad. They drove for hours, down the streets near the Care Center, down back roads between berry fields, but they didn't see Grandpa. Soon it was too dark to see anything.

Finally, Dad drove home. Caleb went to bed reluctantly. He could hear Dad in the next room, talking quietly on the phone, checking police stations, checking hospitals. Caleb tossed and turned. He thought about Grandpa, remembering the great times before Grandpa got sick.

Grandpa used to take Caleb berry picking. They'd fill buckets with wild blackberries, eating as many as they'd pick, munching until their tongues turned purple. Then they'd come back home and boil up jam. Grandpa's jam was a blue ribbon winner at the state fair. Caleb's mouth watered at the memory. He hoped Grandpa was safe somewhere.

He rolled over and punched his pillow into a softer shape.

He thought about fishing. Grandpa loved to fish. "Gonna catch us a mess of trout, boy," he'd tell Caleb. Every Saturday, rain or shine, they'd take Shep down the path to the creek. There was a special spot near the bridge, a spot Grandpa claimed was chock full of the biggest, smartest fish in the county. "But they can't outwit us, boy!" he'd tell Caleb, clapping his shoulder. "Can't beat these two fine fishermen!" They'd fish together all day long until the sun went down.

Toward morning, Caleb drifted off to sleep. Shep snored soundly next to Caleb's bed.

The next day was Saturday. Caleb rode his bike to the Care Center to meet Dad, who had driven over earlier. The head nurse was worried and kind. She and Dad talked and talked. *And all the while,* thought Caleb, *Grandpa's lost.* Maybe he's cold. Maybe he's scared. Maybe he's hungry. And maybe he can't find his way back because he might not even remember who he is.

Caleb sat down outside the front entrance. When they were finished here, Dad was going to drive along the streets again, stopping to knock on people's doors. Caleb and Shep were going to ride down the narrow country lanes. Someone, somewhere, must have seen Grandpa.

An elderly lady wheeled her chair up to Caleb. "You must be Mr. O'Hara's son," she said, her voice thin and shaky.

"No, ma'am," said Caleb. "He's my grandpa."

She paid no attention. Her skin was networked with wrinkles. She was much older than Grandpa, probably the oldest lady Caleb had ever seen. "Did Mr. O'Hara ever get to visit Aunt Lucy, like he wanted?" she asked.

Caleb leaped, electrified. He raced to his father down the hall. "Dad!" he called, tugging on his father's sleeve.

"Just a minute, son." Dad shook him off and continued talking to the nurse.

Caleb couldn't wait. He ran outside and jumped on his bike. Shep raced along beside him. The fishing hole. It had to be. His legs pumped the pedals up and down, up and down, his heart beating in time. He reached the path through the berry field and jumped down, letting his bike crash to the ground. He took off running. Shep followed, his ears bouncing, his tongue hanging out.

Caleb reached the fishing hole by the bridge. Someone was there, slumped against the trunk of the big old oak. "Grandpa!" cried Caleb. Shep barked sharply.

The man turned his head. "Grandpa!" Caleb ran into his arms. "It's me, Caleb."

Grandpa patted his back clumsily. "Yes, yes, I remember. Abe's boy. Caleb. And Shep. Good dog. Gonna catch a mess of trout, boy. Gonna catch Aunt Lucy this time."

Caleb helped Grandpa up the path to the road. Dad was driving by when they got there. Together, they put Grandpa in the car and drove him back to the Care Center.

Later, Caleb and Dad sat in Grandpa's room. The doctor said Grandpa was going to be fine. Now Grandpa lay on his bed, snoring softly. Caleb watched the old man's chest rise and fall under the warm blanket.

"Caleb," said Dad quietly, "what made you think of the fishing hole?"

"It was that lady," said Caleb. "She wanted to know if Grandpa got to visit Aunt Lucy. Grandpa must have said something to her. I remembered that Aunt Lucy was Grandpa's special name for that big old fish we never could catch. So I knew he must be at the fishing hole."

Caleb looked at Grandpa sleeping on the bed. "Dad, when Grandpa's better, let's take him fishing."

Dad nodded. "Good idea, son. We'll do that."

In his sleep, Grandpa smiled.

Skiing Lessons

By Genna S. White

The wind whipped my hair in front of my eyes as the boat made a wide turn, cutting smoothly through the water. I looked behind me, watching Ellen as she skied. She made it look so easy. And fun. As I watched, she lifted one hand in the air and made a circular motion.

"She wants to go around again," I called out to Uncle Stephen.

"OK, once more," he answered, glancing back over his shoulder.

From her seat next to mine, Aunt Gail smiled at me. "We'll let Ellen go around once more, Carrie, then you'll get your turn. Ellen skis all the time, since we come to the lake so often. But you'll only be with us a week. We have to make the most of your time here, right?"

"Right," I said, forcing a smile to my face. I turned my attention back to the water. This visit with my aunt, uncle, and cousin had been my parents' idea. When Mom decided to go with Dad to his convention, Aunt Gail had invited me to spend the week with them at their cabin on the lake. Mom and Dad thought Ellen and I would enjoy being together again. After all, she was thirteen, just a year older than I. And we had once been friends when we were little, spending all our time together during family visits.

But things were different now. Ellen was different. She acted as if she didn't want to be around me. In the past year, we'd seen each other only once, and Ellen had hardly talked to me. This visit looked like more of the same. This was my first day here, and Ellen had pretty much ignored me so far. I'd be glad when the week was over.

Suddenly, Ellen toppled sideways and fell into the water.

"She's down!" Aunt Gail shouted.

Uncle Stephen slowed the boat, turned it around, and headed to the spot where Ellen waited.

"I want to go around again, Dad," Ellen said when we reached her.

"Carrie should have a turn, honey," Uncle Stephen said.

Ellen scowled at me, and I felt my face turning even redder under the hot sun.

"That's all right, Uncle Stephen," I said. "I don't know how to ski anyway."

Ellen gave a hoot of laughter. "I thought you knew everything."

I was silent, confused by her comment.

"Come on, Carrie," Uncle Stephen said. "You're going to love skiing."

Ellen had used only one ski, but since I was a beginner, Aunt Gail gave me two. Then, with advice and instructions from all three of them, I was ready to go.

I didn't even make it to my feet. I just fell forward, face first into the murky water.

"That's all right," Aunt Gail called. "You just keep trying."

Ellen didn't say anything, but I could see she was laughing.

Over and over, I tried and failed. I couldn't get to a standing position, much less ski.

"Come on, Carrie," Ellen said. Exasperation filled her voice.

"I'm trying."

"Well, try harder."

I felt totally embarrassed. I couldn't believe I was having such a hard time. I didn't want to fail at this, especially not in front of Ellen. But my arms and legs weren't strong enough. Time and again, the rope was yanked out of my grasp as the boat moved forward. After a while, I felt drained of energy, my muscles sore.

"It's getting late," Uncle Stephen called. "You want to try one more time?"

I shook my head, defeated. "Maybe tomorrow."

I waited for Ellen to make some comment or laugh at me, but she was silent as I climbed into the boat and we headed back to the dock. She didn't say much to me for the rest of the evening, but I was getting used to that.

The next morning, I woke up early and walked down to the dock. My wrists hurt from trying to ski, but I was determined to learn before the end of the week. I wanted to show Ellen that I could do it.

I was standing there, looking into the water, when I heard quiet footsteps. Ellen came up beside me.

"Hi," she said.

"Hi."

Ellen stared out over the lake. The water was smooth as glass, the early morning sun bouncing off the surface.

"It's nice out here this time of day, isn't it?" Ellen asked.

I looked at her in surprise. This was the first time in a long time that Ellen actually sounded as if she wanted to have a conversation with me.

"It's beautiful," I answered. "You're lucky to be able to come here so often."

"I guess." She paused. "You going to try skiing again today?"

"Sure. My wrists are sore, but that's OK."

Ellen glanced down at my wrists, then looked closer and frowned. "Your wrists are swollen, Carrie. You can't ski like that. You need to wait until the swelling goes down."

I didn't say anything. I had noticed my wrists were a little puffy when I woke up, but I'd hoped it wouldn't last long.

"Tell you what," Ellen said. "We'll do something different today, and give your wrists a chance to recover. Then, when the swelling goes down and they don't hurt anymore, you need to build up the strength of your grip."

"How?"

"I can show you some exercises. Maybe you can try to ski again later on in the week."

I couldn't believe it. Ellen really sounded as if she cared.

"Why are you doing this?" I asked.

"Doing what?"

I shrugged. "Being nice to me. Most of the time lately, you act as if you don't even want me around."

Ellen sat down on the edge of the dock. She squinted up at me for a moment, then shook her head. "I guess I haven't been very nice, have I?"

"Not really."

She was quiet a moment before she spoke. "You don't know what it's like, Carrie. I have to hear about you all the time—what good grades you make, how great you are on the piano, how you're so popular at school. My mom's always talking about you, and I feel like I . . . don't measure up or something."

I stared at her. "But, Ellen, I've got the same problem. Don't you know? My mom tells me all sorts of stuff about you. Like how your pitching took your baseball team to the championship. And you're a whiz at debating, and you're on the staff of the school paper."

"Really?" Ellen gazed into the water for a moment, then looked back at me. "When I hear all the things you're good at, it always sounds as if things are easy for you. But then I saw how hard you were working at learning to ski. I guess I've been wrong about you."

"Some things are kind of easy for me," I said, "but a lot of things aren't. We're good at different things, Ellen, that's all."

"Why did it take me so long to see that?"

I shrugged, and we stared at each other a minute, then burst out laughing.

"Maybe we should have talked about this a long time ago," Ellen said.

"Well, at least we're talking now." For the first time since my visit started, I felt happy. "You think we can be friends again?"

"I'd like that." Ellen grinned and jumped to her feet. "Come on, I'll race you back to the cabin. Dad's making breakfast. I'm starving!"

The rest of the week was a blur of activity and fun. We went hiking and swimming, took boat rides, and went on picnics.

And the day before I left, with Ellen shouting words of encouragement, I skied around the lake.

The Left-Right, Swing-Your-Partner Chicken Dance

By Judy Cox

Adam stared down at his feet. One of them was his left foot. So of course, obviously, the other one was his right. Stupid! Even a kindergarten baby could tell left from right. What was the matter with him?

Megan waited, her fists jammed into her hips, her toe tapping impatiently. The music swept on around them. In Adam's row, the dancers finished swinging their partners and began the first part of the dance again. Adam gave Megan a sheepish shrug and faced front. At least he knew this part. He made his fingers into little beaks and pinched the air three times, flapped his elbows three times, waggled his hips, and clapped three times. Easy as pie. Nothing to it.

Until they got to the swinging part again. The part when he had to link right elbows with Megan and swing her around. He got it right half the time. It was the other half that made her angry. Oops! Wrong way! He felt Megan's foot squash under his each time he turned to the right just as everyone else was going left.

"Mrs. Fernandez!" Megan yelled. "Adam stepped on me. Again!" Mrs. Fernandez stopped the record and pulled Adam off to the side. She tapped his elbow.

"This, Adam, is your left elbow." She bustled up to the front of the class again. "One more time, everybody! Looking good! Only two more days until the program!" She clapped her hands briskly and started the record again. Adam sighed. Now, which elbow had she tapped?

Adam confided his problem to his best friend, Race, on the way home from school. "You worry too much," Race said. "The chicken dance is easy. Good thing you aren't in Olsen's class, like me.

We have to do the varsovienne." Race grabbed his backpack and held it out in front of him. "Point your little foot! Point your little foot! Point your little foot right here!" he sang in a squeaky falsetto, stamping his foot as if he were smooshing ants.

Adam doubled up with laughter.

But that didn't solve his problem. The program was only two days away. His parents would be there and his grandparents. His sister, Cathy, was home from college on spring break and—worst of all—she was bringing her boyfriend, Greg. Greg was on the college basketball team, and he'd promised to show Adam how to dunk the ball. If Adam screwed up at the program, Greg would think he was a nerd. No way would he teach Adam any cool moves.

"Why'd we have to have folk dancing in gym class anyway," Adam grumbled to his parents as he cleared the dinner table.

"Don't you like dancing?" asked Dad in surprise.

"No. Well, yes, a little, I guess. But I don't like Megan for my partner."

"That tall, pretty blond girl?" Mom asked as she rinsed the forks and put them in the dishwasher.

"She's too bossy." Adam didn't want to tell his parents the real trouble was he got right and left mixed up. They'd think he was foolish.

That night, while he was brushing his teeth, he had an idea. He'd wear a watch. You always wear a watch on your left wrist, same as a wedding ring was always worn on the third finger of your left hand. In the morning, Adam carefully checked out Dad and put his own watch on the same wrist. Left. He was all set.

But somehow he must have gotten confused, because when it came time to swing Megan around, he bumped into her, hard, so hard she fell down. "I'm not dancing with that klutz!" she yelled. Everyone turned to look. Adam felt his ears grow hot. One more day until the program.

At dinner, he realized what had happened. He had been facing Dad when he put on the watch. He'd put it on his same wrist. But that was his *right* wrist, of course. Obviously! How dumb could you get!

But it didn't matter anyway, because in his backpack was a paper with directions for the program night. "Dress in good clothes," the handout said. "NO JEWELRY: earrings, bracelets, necklaces, or watches." So the watch was out.

The next morning, Adam woke up with a stomachache. Tonight was the program. Tonight the whole world would know that Adam Metzger was a klutz with a capital K. He dragged his feet on the way to the gym for the last dance rehearsal.

Megan glared at him. "You'd better get it right," she hissed. "My whole family's coming tonight, and I don't want you to make me look bad!"

Adam flushed. He stared down at his shoes. The laces were undone again. He bent to tie them. The laces!

That night, at the program, he felt all twitchy inside as he lined up with his class. Would his plan work? He looked at his feet, the left shoe threaded with an orange lace. "Left, orange," he whispered. Megan narrowed her eyes. The music started. Pinch, pinch, pinch. Flap, flap, flap. The easy part was nearly done. Adam's heart pounded in his throat. The hard part was coming up. Wiggle, wiggle, wiggle. Clap, clap, clap. Here it was.

He glanced quickly down at his shoes, stepped forward with his orange-laced foot, and hooked elbows with Megan. She smiled sweetly and held her petticoat out like Mrs. Fernandez said. It worked!

Adam relaxed. Nearly through now. He smiled at Megan. The music sounded good, and surprise! Dancing was fun! The record finished and the boys bowed, one arm in front, one behind, as they'd been taught. Megan and the girls curtsied. The audience clapped.

"Not bad," whispered Megan. "Thank goodness you didn't mess up!" Adam barely heard. The sound of applause was still sweet in his ears. He'd done it!

After the program, Adam's family came up and congratulated him.

Greg, tall as a skyscraper, put a friendly arm on Adam's shoulder. "Tomorrow we'll shoot some baskets. What do you say, Champ?"

Adam grinned. "Yeah!"

Good Friends

By Helen Kronberg

Kiley and Greg poked along on their way home from school. "It looks like the moving van is gone," Kiley said.

Greg nodded. "Yup. And that's Grandpa's car in our driveway. We're going to sleep at Grandpa and Grandma's house tonight. Tomorrow Grandpa will drive us to the airport." He gulped and wiped a sleeve across his face.

Kiley dug into his pocket. He rubbed his hand slowly over the piece of quartz. Then he handed it to Greg. "Here. You take it."

"That's your favorite!" Greg said. "You're giving me your favorite stone?"

"Remember when we got them?" Kiley said. "Yours is almost exactly like mine. They're a pair, sort of." He bit his lip. "Like you and me."

Greg sniffed. "Thanks." He rubbed his fingers over the small rock as Kiley had done. Then he shoved it deep into his pocket.

"Boys," Kiley's mother called. "Your folks are over here, Greg."

Slowly the boys passed the house that now stood empty. They trudged up the steps to Kiley's house. "Help yourself to snacks," Kiley's mother said.

Greg shook his head and tried to smile. "Thanks. I'm not really hungry."

"Now that the boys are finally back here, we'd better be on our way," Greg's mother said as she rinsed out her coffee cup. In moments Greg and his family were gone.

Kiley rushed off to his room and closed the door. He curled up on his bed and closed his eyes tight. He felt as if his whole life had been poured out. There was nothing left but a deep, dark hole.

Every day going to and from school, Kiley had to walk past Greg's house. Even the house looked drab and lonely.

One day there was another moving van in the driveway. Other people, strangers, were moving into Greg's house.

Kiley ran the rest of the way home. He burst into the house, slamming the door behind him.

"Kiley," his mother said. "What's wrong?"

Kiley slumped onto the couch. "Somebody is moving into Greg's house."

His mother nodded. "Yes, I know."

Kiley stared at her. "You don't care?"

His mother patted Kiley's hand. "The house was sold, Kiley. Greg and his parents won't be back here to live. A house needs people to take care of it. It needs to be lived in."

Kiley sighed. Maybe there would be just grown-ups. Maybe they wouldn't even use Greg's room.

One day a man built a ramp over the front steps. The next day a boy sat in the yard. He was in a wheelchair. Kiley gulped and walked over to him. "Are you gonna live here?" Kiley asked.

The boy smiled. "Yup. My name is Alexander. Call me Lex."

Kiley wanted to tell the boy that he couldn't live here. This was Greg's house. Instead he said, "My name is Kiley. I live next door. My best friend used to live in this house."

"I bet you miss him."

Kiley nodded. "We were best friends almost as soon as we were born. Now he's gone. We talk to each other on the phone. But it's not the same."

"It's hard to move away from your friends," Lex said, looking sad.

Kiley told him about Greg and the things they liked to do. Lex told Kiley about the accident that had put him in the wheelchair. "But I'm getting better fast," he said.

"Tomorrow maybe I could push the wheelchair over to my driveway," Kiley said. "Do you like to shoot baskets?"

Lex laughed. "Sure. I never tried to shoot from a wheelchair. But I may as well give it a try."

The next day Kiley hurried home from school. Lex was waiting.

"I would never make the wheelchair Olympics," Lex said after a few minutes. "You shoot. I'll watch," he said.

Kiley shot a few baskets. Then they sat in the sun at a patio table and played board games.

On chilly or rainy days they played inside at Lex's house. Lex taught Kiley how to play chess.

Kiley was there when Lex left the wheelchair to walk with crutches. And when he could walk without them, they went back to shooting baskets.

"Did you and Greg shoot baskets together a lot?" Lex asked.

"Practically every day when the weather was good enough that we could."

Lex laughed. "No wonder you're good. I won't match you even when my legs are back to normal."

"That's good," Kiley said. "'Cause I'll never beat you at a game of chess if we play for a million years. But it's fun anyway."

Kiley took Lex into his house to show him his rock collection.

Kiley learned how to play a pretty good game of chess. Lex learned about rocks and slowly improved at shooting baskets. And when Lex was strong enough to run, Kiley took him to the ballpark.

"Hey, kids," he said. "This is my new friend. His name is Lex. He lives next door to me, in the house where Greg used to live."

They chose teams, and Lex was put on first base.

"You're really good at baseball," Kiley told him on the way home.

Lex grinned. "I guess we finally found something that we're both good at." He ran a hand through his damp hair. "I've been thinking about your friend, Greg. I hope he's as lucky as I've been."

Kiley nodded. "I think of him a lot. But I don't worry about him anymore. New friends can be good friends, too. And sometimes they teach you stuff you didn't know before. Greg will like that in his new town, too."

Booker T.'s Hiccups

By Christine Henderson

My sister, the pest, stood in the doorway of my room.

"Go away," I said. "I can't practice with you staring at me."

"Why not?" Alisha asked.

"Because you're making me nervous."

"Geoffrey, a whole audience is going to stare at you on Friday."

"Thanks for reminding me," I said.

It took me the rest of that week to learn my lines for my school's Black History Month program.

Alisha read my part on Thursday and memorized it on Thursday.

"I could be in your show," she bragged, smiling.

"That's funny," I said. "I didn't know Mr. Washington was ever a girl."

Friday night, the school auditorium was packed. I couldn't even find my family. While I waited to go on stage, I paced back and forth, saying my lines to myself. I checked my costume in a mirror and saw Alisha standing behind me.

"What are you doing here?" I demanded, turning around to face her.

She grinned. "Mrs. Kelly said I could watch from here, as long as I'm quiet."

"That'll be a miracle," I grumbled.

"Geoffrey, you're next," Sarah told me. She'd just finished her part as Madame C.J. Walker, the first black woman millionaire.

I gulped. "Thanks." I took a deep breath as I walked out on the stage, and then another. Pretty soon I could hear myself breathing. I didn't know it then, but it's not good to swallow too much air.

"My name is Booker T. Washington," I began. "I was born a slave, in Virginia in 1858. I didn't have a last name until I started school after the Civil War. Hic!"

Some kids in the front row giggled. My face felt hot.

"I chose the name Washington. Hic! My middle name is—hic!—Taliaferro."

By now, almost everybody in the room was laughing. I couldn't stop hiccuping, so I had to leave the stage. A few people—my parents, probably—applauded.

Mrs. Kelly didn't look angry. "Sit down here and try to relax," she said.

"I'm sorry I—hic—ruined the show," I gasped.

"You didn't ruin it. I'm sure you would've done fine. Now breathe slowly."

"Mrs. Kelly?" Alisha said. "I know Geoffrey's part. Could I finish it?"

"You can't," I said between hiccups. "You're a girl."

"So? Did Booker T. Washington have a sister?"

"Yes, but—"

"Then I'll be her," Alisha said.

Mrs. Kelly told her to go ahead, and she strolled out to the center of the stage.

There was nothing that I could do about it. I was busy breathing into a paper sack that Mrs. Kelly had found.

"Hello," Alisha said. "I'm Booker T. Washington's younger sister. He wanted to talk to you himself, but he's got the hiccups."

The audience laughed. I groaned and pulled the sack down over my head.

"What he was going to say was that he always wanted an education. He studied hard, and when he was fifteen, he went away to college. He graduated from Hampton Institute and became a teacher there."

"She's really good," Sarah said. Mrs. Kelly nodded. I hated to admit it, but they were right.

"At twenty-three, Booker helped to build a school that trained black men for different kinds of jobs," Alisha continued. "Tuskegee Institute, named after the city in Alabama, is now one of the most important colleges in the nation." She smiled, adding, "Let's give my brother a big hand!"

Talk about embarrassing. But I'd finally stopped hiccuping, so I had to go out. I shook Alisha's hand, then we both took a bow. The audience gave us a big ovation, and that was the end of the program.

"Thanks for being a pest," I told Alisha, smiling.

"Anytime," she said.

Our parents came over to greet us. Dad was holding his camcorder.

"Great show," he said. "I've got it all on tape."

"Can we erase my part?" I asked.

Mom laughed. "It's too bad you can't do it over."

That gave me an idea. "I can. For the camera."

"But the show's over," Alisha said.

"Well, I'm still in my costume, and the stage is here. And I don't have the hiccups."

"Three good reasons," Mom said, smiling.

It wasn't the way I'd planned it. But when I finished my part, I thought that Booker T.—and his sister—would've been proud.

The
Un-Dooming
of
Charles P. Abernathy

By Carolyn Bowman

So, I had a rotten day. It can happen to anyone.

"Start over," Pop said the next morning. "Every day is a new beginning."

What did he know? He hadn't been in the sixth grade for—well—a long time. And he didn't have to show up for class, to face an angry mob. Boy, were they waiting for me, all twenty-three students, in Miss Worthington's room.

They were cool, didn't say a thing, just dropped notes on my desk and sneered at me.

Susan Lee's note said it all: "Charles P. Abernathy, you smell." She was not talking about my gym sneakers.

What did I do to deserve their anger? Let me count the ways.

1. This shouldn't really matter—it was an accident—I spilled a carton of chocolate milk on our class poster for the art show, so we had to start over.

2. I misspelled "calendar" in the schoolwide spelling bee. In all fairness, I didn't ask to be the class representative.

3. The paper airplane I made and launched during math—that made everyone laugh—got us all grounded for a half hour after school. In all fairness, that *was* my fault.

Zeroing in on Pop's approach, I took the first chance to say, "Sorry, guys. Give me a break."

Susan Lee frowned. "Sorry doesn't fry the bacon."

"Yeah," echoed Billy Bathgate. "Sorry doesn't walk the dog."

"Or fly the kite," said Rosemary Watkins.

That was it. My chance to start over, gone right down the tubes. The words of a life sentence hovered in living color above my head: "Charles P. Abernathy, you are doomed."

I stayed doomed through science and social studies. When the bell rang for lunch, I took my classmates' nasty notes to the garbage can. Carrying the weight of so much anger made my elbows ache. I was sure that if I dropped the notes on my foot, they'd break a toe.

Then lunch. You haven't lived or suffered until you've sat through lunch—alone—at the end of a long table, with enough space between you and the next guy to build a moat around a castle. The look Susan was giving me said she would build a moat, if she could, and fill it full of alligators.

You can only stay in a cafeteria for so long. With three students left in the room, I scrammed. There was a calendar in my brain. On it were all the days, weeks, and months until summer vacation. The numbers flew out in front of me down the corridor.

I stopped and stared into the computer room, one of my favorite places in the whole school. Sitting in front of a monitor were the leaders of the newly formed We-Hate-Charles P. Abernathy Club.

"Do I smell a rat?" Susan frowned as I took a seat in front of another computer.

"Forget the rat," said Billy. "We don't have much time left to figure this out."

Rosemary waved a floppy disc. "I don't even know how to load it."

Susan took the disc. "I can load it, but what about the commands?"

Billy stared at the directions. "This is like a foreign language."

"We might as well give up," said Susan. "We'll never win."

"Win what?" I said.

"Don't talk to him," Rosemary said.

Luckily Billy did. "The class that gets the highest score on Math Whiz wins a pizza party. Mr. Jones just told us—he's announcing it right after recess."

So, Mr. Jones, our computer teacher, was holding a contest. "May I borrow your disc for a minute—and the directions?"

Susan frowned, but she handed over the disc.

Popping it into the A drive, I worked through the directions. Math Whiz was organized sort of like a space shuttle game Pop gave me last Christmas, where you use the computer's keyboard to shoot a laser beam on letters in order to make words. There were some minor differences, like shooting numbers instead of letters. In no time at all, I had the program running.

"Hey," Billy said, "you're good at that."

"Let me try," said Rosemary.

"Then me," said Susan.

We were semipros by the time the bell rang. Leaving the computer room, I felt the words of my life sentence of doom float away.

"We can practice some more at my house after school," Rosemary said, "on my computer. You come, too, Charles."

"Yeah," Susan said. "You can teach us more."

"Hey, Charles," said Billy, "thanks."

"No problem," I said. "It just so happens that I love pizza."

HOWDY OATS

By Kim Feerer

"I can speak Spanish," said Christa, pulling her boots on.

"You can?" asked her mother.

"Our teacher taught us yesterday," said Christa. "Howdy oats."

Christa's mother frowned. "What does that mean?" she asked.

"It means good-bye," said Christa, slipping into her jacket. Then she raced out the door. "Howdy oats, Mom," she called.

Christa arrived at school just as Mrs. Cherry called the children to the circle. Christa noticed a new boy with big brown eyes and dark hair.

"We have a new student today," announced Mrs. Cherry. "His name is Arturo. He speaks Spanish and a little English," she explained. "Who will be his friend today?"

Christa waved her hand high. "All right, Christa," Mrs. Cherry said.

Christa showed Arturo what to do at the number center. When it was choosing time, she led him to the plastic bricks. "Do you want one of these?" asked Christa, holding up a brick.

Arturo nodded.

"What color?" she asked. Arturo was quiet.

"Red?"

Arturo shook his head. He pointed to a yellow brick. "Jellow," he said in a quiet voice.

Two boys nearby stopped playing. "Jell-O! Jell-O!" one boy teased. They both laughed. Arturo's face turned red. He threw his bricks down and ran to the paint corner.

"Stop making fun, Jimmy!" cried Christa. Arturo was sitting under the easel, hiding his face. Two big tears gathered in his eyes.

"Arturo, come out," she said. "Here, I brought you a yellow brick."

But Arturo shook his head. So Christa crawled under the easel with him. "I can speak Spanish," she whispered. "Howdy oats."

"Howdy oats?" repeated Arturo, puzzled.

"You know, good-bye," said Christa. "Howdy oats is good-bye in Spanish."

A smile broke out on Arturo's face. "*Adios,*" he said. "Good-bye in Spanish."

"*Adios?*" said Christa. "Well, it sure sounds like howdy oats!" She crawled out from under the easel and stood up. "Want to paint?" she asked.

Arturo stood up next to her and watched. She made a red house. "This is red, see?"

"Red," said Arturo. "*Rojo.*"

Christa repeated the word. "Ro-ho."

Then she painted a blue sky. "How do you say blue?" she asked.

"Blue? *Azul,*" replied Arturo.

"And here's a big yellow sun." Christa made a circle with her brush.

Arturo looked at his feet.

"It's yellow," she said again.

"Y-y-yellow," he said quietly.

"That's right, yellow," said Christa.

"Yellow," repeated Arturo. He started to laugh.

Christa put down her brush. "What's so funny?" she asked.

"Yellow!" cried Arturo. "Yellow in Spanish is . . ." He stopped speaking and looked around. Then he ran to the pitcher of punch from snack time. He pointed to the ice cubes floating in it. "*Hielo!*"

Christa laughed. "I get it. *Hielo* is ice in Spanish!"

Arturo stopped laughing. He saw Jimmy walking toward them.

"Here," said Jimmy. He put a boat made from plastic bricks into Arturo's hand. "I made it for you."

"Thank you," Arturo said in a soft voice. He smiled at Jimmy.

Jimmy, Arturo, and Christa played together until Mrs. Cherry called them to go home.

"*Adios,*" said Christa. "See you tomorrow."

Arturo turned to go. "Howdy oats!" he called.

The
Q and Q
SISTERS

By Harriett Diller

On the day the first snow fell the Q and Q Sisters went to work.

"This mission is top secret," said Annie. "We all know what our job is."

"First stop, Mrs. Bond's house," Sara said. "It's the one on the corner."

"The Q and Q Sisters strike again!" yelled Marly, the third of the girls.

It was still early. They saw few cars and fewer people. At Mrs. Bond's house, the Q and Q Sisters got their secret weapons ready.

"Go!" Annie said in a loud whisper. "And don't forget our motto. Quick and quiet."

The three girls lived up to their name. Within minutes, they had finished the job.

Annie pointed across the street. "Mr. and Mrs. Wayne's house next. Then Miss Arno."

"And don't forget the Gabers," Sara added. "Mr. Gaber broke his leg last week."

"Aye, aye, sir." Marly saluted and marched across the street with her secret weapon over her shoulder.

The Q and Q Sisters worked faster than ever. According to Marly's watch, it was only 7:55 A.M. when they finished.

"Hurry!" Annie cried. "I see Mrs. Gaber coming out the front door!"

In a few moments the Q and Q Sisters had finished their work. They barely managed to scurry out of Mrs. Gaber's sight in time. Crossing the street, the Q and Q Sisters saw Mrs. Bond standing on her front steps with a puzzled look on her face.

"What in the world?" Mrs. Bond stared at the sidewalk in front of her house. "Someone has shoveled my walk. Now who on earth would have done such a nice thing?" Mrs. Bond shook her head. "Whoever it was, they were certainly quiet about it."

The girls did their best to hide their shovels. "And quick, too," said Annie.